A MYSTERY OF
THE
UNDERGROUND

BY

JOHN OXENHAM

British Library Cataloguing-in-Publication Data
A catalogue record for this book is available from the
British Library

CONTENTS

JOHN OXENHAM

John Oxenham was the pen name of William Arthur Dunkerley, born in Manchester, England in 1852. He spent much of his life in Ealing, West London, where he served as deacon and teacher at the Ealing Congregational Church. In the 1920s, became the mayor of Worthing, Sussex. He was a prolific writer, producing more than 40 novels, a number of books of verse, a large body of poetry, and short fiction. His collection *Bees in Amber: A Little Book of Thoughtful Verse* (1913) was a popular bestseller, and he was a major contributor to Jerome K. Jerome's *The Idler* magazine. Oxenham died in 1941, aged 88.

A MYSTERY OF THE UNDERGROUND

JOHN OXENHAM

The underground station at Charing Cross was the scene of considerable excitement on the night of Tuesday, the fourth of November. As the 9.17 London and North-Western train rumbled up the platform, a lady was seen standing at the door of one of the first-class carriages, frantically endeavouring to get out, and screaming wildly.

The station inspector ran up to the carriage, and pulled open the door, when the lady literally sprang into his arms. She was in a state of violent hysterics, and it was with difficulty that he assisted her across the platform to a seat.

Meanwhile, a small crowd gathered round the open carriage door. The guard of the train had come up, elbowed his way through, and entered the carriage. The spectators could see a man sitting in the further corner, apparently asleep, his hat over his eyes, his head sunk forward.

'Drunken brute! he's frightened the lydy!'

'Pitch him out, guard, and we'll jump on 'im!'

The guard shook the man roughly, his hat rolled off, and the crowd jeered.

Then, suddenly, the guard came back to the door, waved his flag to a porter, and said hurriedly:

'Block the line behind – quick – and send the inspector.'

The porter hurried off, shouted to the inspector, and ran down the train to the signal-box.

The inspector left his charge in care of some ladies, and pushed his way into the carriage. The guard said a word to him, and they bent over the man in the corner. Then, with startled faces and compressed lips, after a momentary hesitation, they stopped and lifted him out of the carriage. The head fell back as they carried him awkwardly across the platform, and the crowd shrank away, silent and scared, at sight of the ghastly limpness and the stains of blood.

'Where to?' said the guard.

'Upstairs, I suppose,' said the inspector; and then added: 'Best thing would be to take him right on to Westminster. It's a Scotland Yard job, is this!'

'That's so!' said the guard. 'And her, too?' nodding towards the hysterical lady on the seat.

'Yes. Put him in again, and lock the door. I'll see to her. Tell Bob to keep the line blocked till they get the word from Westminster.'

They put the body back into the carriage, locked the door, and the guard went off to the signal-box, while the inspector took in hand the more difficult task of getting the lady, still in a state of hysterics, back into a carriage.

Finally, he had to have her carried in; he stepped in himself, and the train rolled off through the fog, past the line of scared faces on the platform, into the darkness which led towards Westminster; and the red stern light blinked ghoulishly back at the crowd, and tremulously disappeared up the tunnel like a great clot of blood.

Within seven minutes of the arrival of the train at Westminster, Scotland Yard was in possession of the facts, and of the chief factors in the case – the body – and the lady – by this time in a state of extreme nervous prostration. A couple of detectives were minutely examining the carriage as it sped on its journey, and the traffic on the Underground resumed its normal course.

The morning papers contained a brief announcement of the discovery. The evening papers imaginatively worked up all the details they had been able to obtain, and promoted the item to a prominent position among the day's news, in large type, well spaced out. But with the inquest, held next day, the excitement increased. Briefly, all that was learned was this:

From letters and papers found upon the deceased, the

body was identified as that of Conrad Grosheim, a financier and speculator in the City. The identification was confirmed by Grosheim's clerk, and by the landlady of the room he occupied in King's Road, Chelsea.

The station inspector at Charing Cross and the guard of the train spoke to the finding of the body.

Maud Jones stated that she had had a race to catch the train at Temple station. She was running up towards the second-class carriages when the train started and the inspector flung open the door of a first-class and assisted her in, telling her to change at the next station. She had not noticed anything wrong with the gentleman in the corner – thought he was asleep – remembered his cigarette had slipped from his fingers, and was still smoking on the floor, when suddenly her eyes caught sight of blood dripping from his coat, and it flashed upon her that he was dead. She was so horrified that she nearly lost her senses. Was positive the cigarette on the floor was smoking when she got in. No, she did not smell anything like powder – nothing but the cigarette. The window next to the dead man was up. She touched nothing in the carriage, and got out of it as soon as she could. She was a waitress at Belloni's Restaurant, in the Strand. She had never seen the gentleman before, and was only sorry she had ever set eyes on him at all.

The inspector at Temple station confirmed Miss Jones's

story as to her being put into the carriage.

The ticket porter at Temple station swore positively that no one whatever got out of the train. He had watched the young lady helped into the first-class carriage by the inspector, and there was not a single person on the platform when the train went out, except the inspector. Nobody could possibly have got up the stairs while he was watching. He had snapped the ingress gate as the lady passed through, and had not opened the egress one.

Dr Mortimer stated that he had examined the body, and was of the opinion that death had taken place not more than fifteen minutes, certainly not more than half an hour, before his examination. Cause of death was a bullet through the heart. It had entered the body level and straight, passed through the heart, causing instant death, and was found inside the ribs on the right side of the body. Bullet produced. It was of an unusually conical shape, and by impact with the ribs had been slightly flattened. In its natural shape it would be sharper, almost pointed. There were no signs of singeing or burning on deceased's clothing. The bullet made a clean cut through coat and vest, and did its work. If, as he understood, deceased was sitting in the corner of the carriage facing slightly towards the corner which Miss Jones occupied, the shot must have been fired from the seat exactly opposite where deceased sat.

'Or through the window?' queried the coroner.

'Or through the window,' granted the doctor. 'The exact spot from which the shot was fired would depend upon the angle at which deceased was sitting, but I understood the window was found closed.'

'Could the wound have been self-inflicted?'

'It could, of course, but not without singeing the clothing.'

'Could deceased have shot himself, thrown the revolver out of the window, and raised the window?'

'Absolutely impossible; death was instantaneous.'

Miss Jones, recalled, stated that the window was up when she entered the carriage. She was quite certain of that. It was a close, muggy night, and she felt half-suffocated. The window nearest her was jammed, and she could not let it down. She had looked across at the other, and thought of trying to open it. Then she saw the cigarette smoking on the floor, and then she saw the blood, and then she remembered screaming.

Detective-Sergeant Doane, of Scotland Yard, stated that the case had been placed in his hands; that he had taken possession of the carriage within a few minutes of the discovery of the body. It had been examined most minutely by himself and a colleague, both inside and out. Beyond the cigarette, trampled flat, probably in the removal of the body, and a few drops of blood on the floor, nothing whatever had been found. There was no weapon, no sign of a struggle. The contents of deceased's pockets, including a valuable watch and chain, had not been touched. He had questioned the passengers in the next compartments, but no one had heard a shot, or any sound whatever, except the screams of Miss Jones. Further stated that if Miss Jones was correct in stating that the cigarette was still burning on the floor when she entered, and he had no reason to doubt it, he judged that the deed was committed in the tunnel between Mansion House and Blackfriars, and he arrived at it thus. A cigarette of that brand would burn on the floor for five minutes; the train took one and a half minutes to travel from Temple to Charing Cross, half a minute's stoppage at Temple; two minutes from Blackfriars to Temple, half a minute's stoppage at Blackfriars took them into the tunnel between Mansion House and Blackfriars, and there the shot must have been fired. That tunnel had been searched inch by inch, so had the others, but nothing whatever had been found. He had his own ideas on the subject, but declined at present to make them public. Deceased's ticket was from Mansion House to Sloane Square.

The jury returned a verdict of wilful murder against some person or persons unknown; and so one more was added to the long list of undiscovered crimes of the Metropolis.

(From the *Link*, 12 November 1894)
ANOTHER MURDER ON THE UNDERGROUND
THE *LINK* MAN ON THE SPOT, AS USUAL

At 9.21 exactly, last night, as the weary *Link* man, having finished his appointed tasks, was patiently travelling in an Underground train to his humble abode at Chelsea, a piece of great good fortune befell him. Great good fortune to one man generally means corresponding bad fortune to some other man, and so it was in this case. Without desiring to appear over-presumptuous, it does seem providential, that is, to the readers of the *Link*, that the *Link* man was right on the spot, and is therefore able to give an eye-witness's account of the very strange occurrence which took place at St James's Park station on the Underground railway last night.

Our contemporaries have published more or less garbled versions of the matter. They have done their best. The *Link*, however, was the only paper actually represented, and able, therefore, to give an absolutely exact account of what happened.

The *Link* man entered the train at Blackfriars, travelling third-class, as usual. He always travels third – not, as you might imagine, from necessity, but from choice. He thereby sees and feels, and, in every sense of the word, comes so much more in contact with his fellows, than is possible in the cold, refined, varnish-and-saddlebag atmosphere of the first-class. After standing patiently past three stations, the *Link* man had just managed to gently insinuate his person into the sixth place on a seat intended for five, and was jocularly remarking to his scowling neighbours, upon portions of whom he was sitting, that the tighter you sat the less you joggled, when a series of piercing screams from the next carriage forward rent the darkness of the tunnel, and heated all the *Link* man's professional instincts to boiling point. He sprang to the door. Something was happening – something untoward and out of the common. Such screams – off the stage – were an outrage, or implied one.

His first intention was to climb along the footboard till he arrived at the screams. But thoughts of Mrs *Link* man and all the little *Link* men and women deterred him, and he decided not to risk his precious life, but to be first on the scene, all the same.

The screams had ceased. The silence seemed even more pregnant. While the screams continued something was happening. With their cessation, it – whatever it was – had happened. As the train slowed up at St James's Park, the *Link* man dashed forward to the next carriage – the rearmost first-class – and this is what he saw on opening the door – a lady lying apparently lifeless in the corner seat nearest

the platform, and on the floor face downwards, the body

of a man.

A crowd rushed to the door almost as soon as the *Link* man, but his were the first eyes that witnessed the scene. The station inspector came up, and was for ordering the *Link* man away, but, upon the latter disclosing his identity, became the courteous official the *Link* man has always found him, except upon that one unfortunate occasion when he (the inspector) found him (the *Link* man) riding first with a third-class ticket, and only let him off imprisonment for life with a reprimand, which still tingles in the *Link* man's ears, on the *Link* man's proving to him by ocular demonstration that every third-class carriage was carrying thirty per cent more humanity than it had any right to do.

The guard came up, too, and *ex officio*, the *Link* man was privileged to share the labours and cogitations of these officials.

By virtue of her sex, the lady claimed their first attention. She was in a dead faint, and was carefully carried through a double line of curious faces by the *Link* man and the guard to one of the station seats.

The *Link* man left the guard in charge, and hurried back to the carriage.

The inspector was stooping over the prostrate man, and as the *Link* man stepped in, he looked up with scared face, and said, 'It's another murder!'

'Good God!' said the *Link* man, involuntarily, for this was getting exciting. Then he saw blood on the inspector's hands.

'Better block the line behind, and wire to Scotland Yard, hadn't you?' he suggested.

'It blocks itself,' said the inspector; 'but we'll make doubly sure. Stop here in charge, will you, and I'll wire Scotland Yard at same time.' And he went off at a run, leaving the *Link* man in full charge.

Notebook and pencil came out of their own accord, with the following results: 'First-class carriage No. 32. London and North-Western train, St James's Park; time 9.25 p.m. Body dressed in dark grey overcoat with velvet collar – dark trousers – black diagonal coat and vest – patent leather shoes – Lincoln and Bennet hat, bruised from a fall. Face, so far as visible, dark and pale – age about forty-five – four-coil snake ring, with ruby and diamond in head, on third finger of left hand. In vest, exactly over heart, small, clean-cut hole, no singeing or burning, no smell of powder – no signs of struggle – window furthest from platform closed. Note – Exactly a week, to the minute almost, since discovery of the murder at Charing Cross last week. Is this accident or horrible intention?'

Link man acknowledges to creepy feeling. Door opens. Inspector returns, and a few minutes later, Scotland Yard, in the person of quiet, stern-faced Detective-Sergeant Doane, who has the previous case in hand, arrives with a colleague. They examine carriage minutely, inside and out, rear-side and off-side, under and over. They say little, but make many notes.

Carriage is locked up, and train sent on. *Link* man notices that most carriages are about half as full as when train came in, as though many had conceived sudden distaste for underground travel – that no single travellers are to be seen – general mistrustful gregariousness observable. *Link* man feels himself that sooner than travel in a carriage alone, or with only one other person, he would stop on the platform all night, and sleep on Smith's bookstall.

Body is carried to ambulance. Lady, now reviving, is placed in cab, and all drive off to Scotland Yard.

The unfortunate victim of this second outrage has since been identified as George Villars, commercial traveller, residing at West Kensington. The lady is Mrs Corbett, manageress of the ABC shop in Albert Street, Westminster.

Her account is simply that she entered the train at Westminster, and had barely got seated when the gentleman opposite lurched forward in his seat, presumably with the shaking of the carriage, and then fell prone on the floor. She saw blood on the floor, and screamed, and then fainted.

What may be the meaning of this exact repetition of the

murder at Charing Cross exactly a week ago it is impossible to say. The time, the manner, the general conditions, are as nearly as possible identical.

Are both murders the act of the same hand; or is Number Two but one more proof of the epidemic nature of abnormal crimes – the result, in fact, of the action of Crime Number One on some weak intellect, with a morbid craving for notoriety?

One thing is certain: travel on the Underground is less attractive than of yore, and the homely 'bus is rising in public estimation.

(From the *Daily Telephone*, 19 November 1894)
A THIRD MURDER ON THE UNDERGROUND

The appalling discovery last night at Ealing Broadway station, on the District Railway, places beyond possibility of doubt the fact that a cold-blooded murderer is at large in our midst, and that travellers on that at all times depressing line are completely at his mercy. The police, we are willing to believe, are doing their best in the matter, but so far their efforts have apparently been fruitless. Every Tuesday night for the last three weeks, at, as near as can be told, exactly the same time to the minute, the mysterious death-dealer has chosen his victim, fired his fatal shot, and vanished.

Whatever his motive and whatever his method, he has succeeded in instilling such a sense of dread into the public mind that the District Railway is beginning to be shunned by all persons of nervous temperament.

This curious state of things recalls to mind a similar series of crimes perpetrated on the Ceinture Railway, in Paris, about seven years ago. There, too, the victims were smitten down by an undiscoverable hand, and it was only when the seventh had fallen that the slaughter stopped. If it had not, the traffic on that line would have ceased, for the excitement was indescribable, and travellers shunned the Ceinture Railway as they would a pest-house.

Much the same feeling is growing in the minds of travellers by the District Railway, and especially so on Tuesday nights, which is the time fixed by the mysterious one for his horrible work. Last Tuesday night the trains ran nearly empty. Numbers of people, so curious is the hankering of the morbid mind after sensation, gathered in the stations most likely to afford the chance of a thrill. The platforms at Charing Cross, Westminster, St James's Park and Victoria were crowded with sensation-seekers, who had taken tickets which they had no intentions of using, but simply with the idea of being on the spot in case anything happened. And a very curious study those platforms were.

Throngs of people, waiting silently, in a damp fog, peering

into carriage after carriage as the almost empty trains rolled slowly, like processions of funeral cars, in and out of the stations. In one carriage a party of young roughs had ensconced themselves, and endeavoured to make things lively by chaffing and jeering the silent crowds on the platforms as they passed through. They met with no encouragement, however, and had things all their own way. We wonder how those lively youths feel now when they know that, beyond a doubt, the mysterious murderer looked in on them, and could, had he so chosen, have launched his deadly bullet into their midst. But, as usual, his fatal choice fell upon a solitary wayfarer occupying a corner seat in a carriage by himself, and within three compartments of one occupied by the rowdy gang referred to.

Many of the crowd on the stations remarked on the temerity of the occupant of that corner seat. He might well sit so quiet. The fatal bullet was in his heart before he reached Victoria, at all events. But he journeyed peacefully on until he reached Ealing Broadway station, the terminus of the line. There, one of the principal duties of the porters is to arouse all the passengers who have succumbed to the monotony of the journey from the City and there John Small, the Ealing porter, tried in vain to arouse Carl Groeb, the occupant of the corner seat in the rear compartment of one of the first-class carriages, and found him dead – murdered, in the same way, and, beyond all doubt, by the same hand which struck down Conrad Grosheim, at, or about, 9.15 on the evening of Tuesday, the fourth inst., at Charing Cross, and which struck down George Villars, at 9.15 on the evening of Tuesday, the eleventh inst., at St James's Park.

The crowds at the stations up the line had dispersed with a sigh of disappointment, or let us take a charitable view, and say of relief. But the tragedy was there all the same, and the victim had passed beneath their eyes, though the public had to wait till Wednesday morning to get its thrill.

It is a terrible fact, but one that has to be faced that, in the greatest city in the world, in this year of grace 1894, such an appalling series of crimes can be perpetrated with impunity.

The police seem powerless. We give them credit for doing their utmost, but, up to now, nothing, so far as they let it be known, has resulted from their efforts.

One thing is certain, if the criminal cannot be brought to justice the directors of the District Railway can close up their line. It would pay them to run the electric light through every tunnel, and to line the route and sprinkle the carriages with detectives, in the style of an Imperial progress in Russia. The matter is really too gruesome for a jest, but *Punch* certainly hit the case off admirably in Bernard Partidge's clever sketch of the young City man attracting all the attentions of all the beauties in the drawing-room by the simple assertion that he had travelled from town by the District Railway, in a first-class carriage, *all by himself,* while the season's lions scowl at him from a distance, and twirl their moustaches, and growl in their neglected corners.

While, in another portion of the same journal, Mr Anstey's 'Voces Populi', describing the scene at Victoria station on Tuesday night, while the crowds waited for what they feared, and made simple bets on the basis of murder or no murder, and more complicated ones as to the age and nationality of the expected victim, the station where the discovery would be made, and so on, is immensely clever, but grim in the extreme. It proves the identity of one of the crowd at all events, and it will afford matter for much wondering comment on the part of readers of this year's *Punch* twenty years hence.

To return to the facts which confront us, however. Murder, grim, cold, calculating, glides unchecked in our midst. No man's life is safe. You yourself, reading this, may be the next victim – that is, if you are so unwise as to trust yourself alone in a carriage on the District Railway. And this in London, AD 1894! What a satire on our boasted civilisation!

The official report of this latest crime is, with the necessary alterations of names, places, and dates, a mere duplication of the previous ones.

Carl Groeb took ticket at Mansion House for Victoria on

the evening of Tuesday, the twenty-fifth inst., at 9.20. Before he reached Victoria he was dead – shot through the heart, in identically the same manner as the previous victims, and not a trace of the murderer is discoverable.

It is beyond belief, and yet it is horrible fact.

(From the *Daily Telephone*, 23 November 1894)

More light has been thrown on the dark corners of the Underground railway during the last few days than at any period of its existence, and yet the mystery remains unsolved. Travellers between 9 and 10.30 p.m. have been few and far between. Indeed, between those hours the service has been almost suspended, not more than one train in ten being run, and that running practically empty. But such hardy voyagers as have ventured, at risk of their lives, to run the passage from the City to Earl's Court, have travelled through a torchlight procession. Every tunnel has been filled with men with flare-lights, and the grotesque effects of the continuous blaze and the weird gigantic shadows are things to be remembered for a lifetime.

Not only is traffic on the Underground disorganised – business and pleasure alike are interrupted in their regular courses. Never, during the last twenty years, has London worked itself up into such a state of excitement as it has done over these mysterious crimes on the Underground. Suburban residents find words even of the most cerulean hue quite inadequate to express the annoyance and inconvenience they are being put to.

Scotland Yard has had a detective patrolling the footboard of every train. This, however, is to be stopped. The sensation of suddenly finding a strange face peering in at your ear as you sit harmlessly reading your evening paper in your favourite corner seat, is enough to startle any man. It has given rise to some most ludicrous scenes. Going home in a Richmond train last night, the writer sat opposite to a quiet, nervous-looking old gentleman. He happened to raise his eyes from his paper just as the patrol on the footboard passed the window. The old gentleman made up his mind at once that he had been selected as the murderer's next victim, and that the deadly bullet was just about to be launched. He instinctively sheltered his head behind his newspaper, and sank suddenly off his seat, and remained flat on the floor, nor could he be induced to rise till the next station was reached. Many ladies have been driven into hysterics in the same way, and the patrols are to be abolished.

In connection with the murder of Carl Groeb, it is now proved beyond doubt that the murderer has added to his other crime the meaner one of robbery. Groeb's pockets were empty when he was discovered – money, watch, chain, all were gone, though the evidence is conclusive that, when he left his office in Houndsditch, he carried a good round sum, and wore a good gold watch and chain. There is more hope of catching the murderer if he is driven by the exigencies of want, or the desire for gain, to unite the functions of footpad with those of self-constituted executioner. At all events, he descends from the sphere of the supernatural, into which popular credulity has been inclined to elevate him, and becomes a mere murderous thief.

(From the *Daily Telephone*, 25 November 1894)

We have received the following letter:

To the Editor of the *Daily Telephone*.

SIR, – You are wrong. I never touched the money or effects of Carl Groeb, or any other of my victims. I kill; I do not rob. – Yours truly,

The Underground Murderer.

The letter is post-marked 'London, SE, 24 November, 1894'. Is it a grim jest, or is it a genuine document? We give it for what it is worth.

The Mystery of the Underground

(From the *Daily Telephone*, 26 November, 1894)

To the Editor of the *Daily Telephone*.

SIR, – The Underground Murderer has enough on his conscience. He did *not* rob Carl Groeb of his watch, chain and money. I did. I entered the carriage at Sloane Square. The attitude of the figure in the corner startled me. When we had passed South Kensington I spoke to him. He did not answer. I touched him. He did not move. I saw he was dead. I was stone-broke myself. I had bilked the ticket-man at Sloane Square, and intended doing the same at Earl's Court. The opportunity was too good to be missed. The man in the corner had no further use for his money. I had. I relieved him of it, and also of his watch and chain. The latter I pawned in Liverpool, and I enclose you the ticket. I am a bad lot, but, thank Heaven, I am

(Signed) Not the Underground Murderer.

The above letter was received by us two days ago, post-marked 'Liverpool'. We sent the pawn-ticket on to Liverpool. The watch and chain, recovered from the pawnbroker, have been sent to London, and have been identified beyond all doubt as Carl Groeb's!

Both letters are in possession of the police.

The Mystery of the Underground

(From the *Daily Telephone*, 27 November 1894)

What, in Heaven's name, is this monstrous thing that is waging cruel, remorseless and indiscriminate warfare with that section of London that travels by the Underground? Is it against the Underground railway itself, as a system or as a corporation, that this foul fiend is fighting? Or is it some lunatic registering in this gruesome fashion his protest against the influx of foreigners into English business life? – for it is a noticeable fact that three out of the four victims have been foreigners.

Last night was 'Murder Night', as Tuesday night has come to be grimly dubbed on the Underground, and two more victims fell to the assassin's bullet – one in the usual neat and finished style to which we are becoming accustomed, but with a change of locality, necessitated, no doubt, by the close and incessant watch kept on every corner of the murderer's old haunts; the other was a gratuitous slap in the face – or, to be precise, bullet in the leg – of one of the guardians of the public safety in charge of the tunnel between Victoria and Sloane Square.

As the train which left Mansion House at 9.16, and left Victoria at 9.31, was running through the tunnel between Victoria and Sloane Square, it passed an up-line train proceeding to Mansion House.

The flare-light men are mostly concentrated between Victoria and Mansion House, in the tunnels of which section all the murders have hitherto been committed. As a precautionary measure, however, half a dozen men have been told off for duty each night in the tunnel between Victoria and Sloane Square. As the two trains passed, one of the flare-men standing in the six-foot fell to the ground, shot through the leg. No report was heard. Nothing but the rattle of the passing trains, which drowned the man's groans as he sank to the ground. His mate down the line saw a blaze of light as his flare fell over, and the oil caught fire and spread along the ground. Running up, he dragged the wounded man away from the flames, and yelled to the other men further down the tunnel.

Among them they carried this latest victim up to Victoria station, where their arrival caused a stampede of all except the officials.

The men's accounts of the matter are confused.

The bullet, of course, came from one of the passing trains, but which they cannot say. Even the wounded man is not certain how he was standing when the bullet struck him, but in any case only the very promptest action could have thrown any light on the matter. Had the men promptly wired to the next stations, both up and down the line, at which both trains would stop, strict search might have led to some discovery. But their wounded mate absorbed all their attention, and the chance, such as it was, was lost. We may, however, conclude, without doubt, that the shot came from the down train. That train reached Baker Street at 9.58, and four minutes later the murderer's fifth victim was discovered in a first-class carriage at Gower Street, in the person of John Stern, merchant, of Jewin Street, who was discovered shot through the heart, in exactly the same way as all the previous victims of the Underground fiend.

How much longer this state of matters is to continue depends, apparently, entirely on the will of the mysterious and bloodthirsty perpetrator of these atrocious crimes. The arm of the law seems powerless. It only remains now for the Underground fiend to shoot down an engine driver and his mate to bring about a catastrophe too horrible to contemplate. The bare possibility of an Underground train deprived of its natural controllers, and crashing madly along at its own sweet will, is enough to make one forswear for ever the delights of travel on that much-maligned line.

(From the *Link*, 4 December 1894)
ANOTHER OUTRAGE ON THE UNDERGROUND
THE *LINK* MAN THE SIXTH VICTIM

To all intents and purposes, I am a dead man.

To all intents and purposes, I am victim No. Six of the Underground Demon.

That I am here alive to tell the tale is no fault of his, but is due to a little precautionary measure of my own.

I have passed through a very strange experience.

I have done what no other man has done. I have looked Death in the face – the Death of the Underground. I have looked down the barrel of the weapon with which the Underground Death-dealer slaughters his victims.

I myself was the victim.

I am free to confess that I am shaken in nerves and sorely bruised in body.

After the detailed account given below of my experiences last 'Murder Night' I have done with the matter. I have had enough of it. My constitution cannot stand the exigencies of up-to-date travel on the Underground. The facts I am about to relate are so passing strange, that I may state at once that they are vouched for by the one man who has had more to do with the Underground Murders (except, of course, the chief actor of all) than anyone else – Detective-Sergeant Doane, of Scotland Yard. Sergeant Doane, into whose hands, from the first, has been entrusted the discovery of the mysterious murderer, has been greatly exercised by the failure of all the ingenious plans laid for his capture, and the apparent impossibility of coming to grips with the invisible one.

It is obviously impossible to have a detective on the step of every carriage of every train on the Underground railway. It is impossible to line the whole length of the system with flare-light men, even on 'Murder Night'. As a matter of fact, since the shooting of John Cran, the flare-man, in Sloane Square tunnel, it is not easy to induce the men to undertake the duty at all, for every one of them feels that he takes his life in his hand when he picks up his lamp. Every man of them knows that, as like as not, he may be the next victim.

I came into contact with Sergeant Doane over the second murder, the one at St James's Park, as readers of the *Link* will remember. I have met him many times since, and we have discussed the matter from many points of view.

On Saturday last I laid before him a scheme which seemed to me to offer at least the chance of a solution of the mystery.

My proposition was this: I offered to take my place, alone, in a first-class compartment in the train leaving Mansion House at 9.12 on 'Murder Night,' and to afford the Underground Fiend every facility for selecting me as his next victim. As a precaution, I was to wear inside my waistcoat a breastplate of solid steel; I was to have the company of an armed detective beneath the opposite seat within reach of a kick, and on top of the carriage, lying flat on the roof, directly over each window of my compartment, were to be two other detectives.

Sergeant Doane turned this idea over in his mind before cautiously venturing the remark that it might do – might do for me, in any case, he grimly added.

The idea was carried out precisely as given above, and 9.13 last Tuesday night found me comfortably ensconced, steel breastplate and all, in the rear first-class compartment of the London and North-Western train from Mansion House to Willesden, gliding through brilliant tunnel after tunnel into the comparative obscurity of the stations, and patiently waiting to be shot at. Beneath the opposite seat, within easy reach of my toe, was one of Doane's trusty followers, armed with a revolver. Flat on the roof, feet to engine, and head over my window, with the cold night wind ploughing up his back hair, was Sergeant Doane himself and over the opposite window another of his men, both armed with revolvers. A slight iron framework had been fixed to the top of the carriage to prevent their rolling off.

Now, a scheme of this kind – I speak from experience – is all very well in the heat of inception and preliminary discussion, but, in the carrying out of it, one's temperature is apt to fall.

I must confess to feeling distinctly nervous as I took my seat in the carriage, and, as the train rumbled along through the weird, irregular illumination of the flarelight men, an odd idea grew upon me that the compartment I was sitting in was somehow unpleasantly familiar to me.

The sensation grew, and the feelings of discomfort increased in proportion. It was likely enough I had ridden in that same carriage dozens of times, for I use the Underground freely, and occasionally go 'first' when, in my opinion, the 'thirds' are full. I was arguing myself into the idea that it was just the natural nervousness incidental to the job I had in hand, when my eye, roving around, caught the number of the carriage – No. 32 – on the small enamelled plate above the door, and I experienced all the sensation of a cold douche down the spine.

'Nonsense!' said I to myself. 'Don't be an idiot!'

But I sat and stared at that small enamelled plate till it began to hypnotise me.

To prove myself a fool, and disperse the blue devils, I hauled out my notebook, and turned over the pages till I came to what was in my mind. And then – I had a strong inclination to get out of the carriage, and have done with the business.

I was sitting in the exact spot of the very compartment of the very carriage in which George Villars was shot exactly five weeks ago to the day, and almost to the minute. As readers of the *Link* will remember, I was the first to discover his body at St James's Park station. It was distinctly unpleasant, but it could not be helped.

For companionship's sake, I landed a kick on a tender portion of the recumbent detective under the seat opposite, and he grunted wakefully. Then, feeling deucedly uncomfortable, I sank my head down into the pose of a tired man, drew my hat down over my brow, and turned my eyes almost upside down in the endeavour to keep a bright look-out from under the brim of it.

Blackfriars, Temple, Charing Cross, Westminster, St James's, Victoria, Sloane Square: I heaved a sigh of relief. We were through the original murder zone, and looked like drawing blank this time. Still, as the murderer had broken fresh ground at Baker Street last week, there was no knowing where he might strike this time. And so the train rumbled on.

Earl's Court, and tickets; Addison Road, Uxbridge Road, Shepherd's Bush, and we were rushing across the wilds of Wormwood Scrubs, when my eyes, wearied almost to blindness with the unnatural strain, closed for a moment's rest.

When I opened them, to my amazement, the window on my left, which I had carefully closed, was down, and wind and rain were pouring in. It sank to the bottom. Every drop of blood in me was tingling with excitement. My heart was going like a sledge-hammer. I wanted to kick the man under the seat, but could not move a toe.

As I glanced at the window, along the polished framework of the part that slides down, there came gently and silently into view a shining steel barrel, pointing straight for my heart. I caught just one vague glimpse of a face beyond it, then – without any report, or any warning, an awful shock – and – blank.

They tell me that I was lifted out at Willesden, and that I was unconscious for upwards of four hours.

I take their word for it; at present I will take anybody's word for anything. As far as I am personally concerned, I have done with the Underground Murders. I hold a season ticket on that abnormal line from Blackfriars to Sloane Square. Anyone who wants it, and will take it with all risks, including its non-transferability, is welcome to it. I would suggest that whoever takes it, should also take out a £10,000 Life Policy for the benefit of his widow and children.

For myself, as I said at the beginning. Underground travel is not adapted to my peculiar constitution. I now go home by 'bus.

As this story is passing strange, and may, in some quarters, be received with incredulity, Sergeant Doane has very kindly offered to add a few words concerning his experiences on Tuesday night.

If any of my fellow-journalists desire ocular demonstration

of the truth of my story, and will call at St Bartholomew's Hospital, they can see for themselves the documents in the case, viz.: one steel shield, and one journalist, with a bruise, of the dimensions of a soupplate, round about the spot where his heart is supposed to be.

Sergeant Doane's account is as follows:—

'I have read the foregoing statement, and endorse it in every particular which came under my own knowledge. Journeying on one's stomach, stern foremost, on top of the Underground train, is not a mode of locomotion that I can recommend. The motion of the train, much more violent up there than in the body of the carriage, the peculiar position, and the horrible atmosphere, produced a feeling of nausea to such an extent that my colleague, on the other side of the roof, when he descended at Willesden, was white as a sheet, and was practically in the throes of sea-sickness.

'Nothing happened on our journey till we reached Wormwood Scrubs. It was blowing half a gale. The heavy rain stung like pellets, and, combined with the rattle of the train, drowned every other sound.

'Half-way between Wormwood Scrubs station and Willesden Junction, the gale seemed to seize the train and shake it, and it was all we could do to hang on by main force. It was at that moment that I heard a shout in the carriage below; then my colleague, Detective Trevor, who had been hidden under the seat, put his head through the window, shouting, "Doane, Doane, he is shot." Half a minute more, and we ran into Willesden station. Mr Lester was insensible from the impact of the bullet, which was flattened on the shield like a shilling. I heard no report, and feel sure there was none. Trevor confirms this fact. Beyond the "ping" of the bullet on the shield, he heard nothing. On hearing that, however, he crawled out, found Mr Lester with all the breath knocked out of him, and yelled for me.'

(From the *Daily Telephone*, 10 December 1894)

We feel like accessories before the fact – like partners in the horrible work of the Underground Murderer.

Ten days ago we hinted in these columns at the appalling catastrophe which might result from the massacre of an Underground engine driver and his mate by the Underground Murderer.

Last night, William Johnson, driver of the 9.1 Outer Circle train, was shot at and wounded, fortunately not fatally, as the train ran through the tunnel beyond South Kensington station.

When the train steamed into Gloucester Road station, it was seen at once that something was wrong. Charles Jones, the fireman, was hanging on to the brake lever, white as a sheet, shouting for help. As the train came to a stand, and the inspectors and guard ran up, Driver Johnson was found lying in a heap on the floor of the cab.

Jones explained hurriedly that, as they ran through the tunnel Johnson suddenly clapped his hand to his side, and cried, 'My God! I'm shot!' and fell all of a heap.

'I'm off,' said Jones, when he had finished his story. I'll have no more o' this – a man's life isn't safe.' Neither threats nor persuasion availed to induce him to resume his place on the engine. Another driver and fireman were eventually procured from Mansion House, and traffic was resumed.

Matters, however, have come to a pretty pass when such an occurrence is possible, and something has got to be done, and at once, to put an end to this unheard-of state of affairs.

The following proclamation has been posted broadcast over the Metropolis. May it have some effect:—

£1,000 REWARD

WHEREAS, on the night of Tuesday, 4 November 1894, Conrad Grosheim was murdered in a first-class carriage on the Underground railway between Mansion House and Charing Cross stations; and

WHEREAS on the night of Tuesday, 11 November 1894, George Villars was murdered in a first-class carriage on the Underground railway between Mansion House and

Westminster Stations; and

WHEREAS, on the night of Tuesday, 18 November Carl Groeb was murdered in a first-class carriage on the Underground railway between Mansion House and Victoria stations; and

WHEREAS, on the night of Tuesday, 25 November John Cran was shot in the leg in the tunnel between Victoria and Sloane Square stations on the Underground railway; and, on the same night, John Stern was found murdered, in a first-class carriage at Baker Street station; and

WHEREAS, on the night of Tuesday, 2 December Charles Lester was shot at and wounded, with intent to murder, while travelling in a first-class carriage between Wormwood Scrubs and Willesden; and

WHEREAS, on the night of Tuesday, 9 December William Johnson, engine-driver, was shot at and wounded, with intent to murder, while travelling on his engine, between South Kensington and Gloucester Road station on the Underground railway:

The sum of ONE THOUSAND POUNDS (£1,000) will be paid to any person or persons (not being the actual murderer or murderers) who shall give such information as shall lead to the detection of the perpetrator of the above deeds.

The above emanated from Scotland Yard. The chairman

of the District Railway Company authorises us to state that his company will double the government reward for information.

(From the *Link*. Third Edition. Wednesday,
12 December 1894)

The £1,000 reward seems to have had its effect. Last night was 'Murder Night' on the Underground, and, for the first time in six weeks, we have no murder to chronicle.

Is the Underground Fiend sated with blood – or, having accomplished the magical number 'Seven', has he retired, satisfied with his work?

Time will show. The terrible chain, however, is broken, and from this we may draw some slight hope that the reign of terror on the Underground is over – until such time as the Death-dealer chooses to resume his self-imposed duties.

Receiving a tip-off that a man believed to be the Underground Murderer is about to flee the country on a boat sailing for Australia, the Link *man Charles Lester joins the vessel, the* Bendigo. *During the following weeks at sea two more murders are committed before Lester finally narrows down the suspects to the most unlikely passenger on board: an old man named Hood who is travelling with his pretty young grand-daughter. When the murderer strikes a third time, however, and tries to kill the ship's doctor, Shannon, who has also become increasingly suspicious of the old fellow, the medical man defends himself with an iron bar and causes his adversary to fall down a stairway to his death. As soon as the news of the old man's death is conveyed to his grand-daughter she is overwhelmed with relief, having apparently been an unwitting accomplice to the reign of terror on the London subway and at sea. After Hood's body has been committed to the ocean, Charles Lester is summoned by Miss Hood to the cabin that had been occupied by her grandfather and there he finally learns the secret of the Underground mystery . . .*

The girl was kneeling on the floor, amid piles of books, papers, clothing, etc., which she had taken from his boxes.

She beckoned me inside, and bade me close the door.

'You have a right to see some of these things, Mr Lester,' she said. 'When you have seen all you care to, will you help me to get rid of them? I only learned this morning from Captain Joram that you were the Mr Lester who—' She faltered, and the large eyes, turned pathetically up to mine, were swimming with tears.

'Try and forget all about it,' I said, 'and let me help you.'

She stooped hurriedly, and picked up a bundle of papers.

'Read those – and those – and look at these,' putting into my hand some strange steel instruments, quite unlike anything I had ever seen before. One had a horse-shoe clutch at the end, and, at the other extremity, it was pinned on to another long, thin steel rod, one end of which terminated in four fine sharp teeth, like the prongs of a fork.

I turned it over in my hand, but could make nothing of it, so proceeded to look over the papers. And, reading them, I arrived at old Hood's story.

A mechanical engineer, of quite unique powers, he had patented a number of inventions, and offered them to the District Railway Company, in whose employment he had spent the best part of his life. Nothing had come of them, however, and I gathered from some of the company's letters in reply that the old man had accused them of using his ideas, but giving him no benefit of them. Then he left the company's service, with his brain bursting with grievances, and it was easy to conceive that he determined to strike at them in a way that was as horribly effective as it was, for him, easy of accomplishment.

I was puzzling over the strange implements, and trying to get at their use. In thought, I went back to one of the murderer's journeys along the swinging footboards, and suddenly it all flashed upon me. A long steel rod, with curved top – that hitched on to the edge of the carriage roof, and had enabled him to pass rapidly along, without troubling to grasp each handle. That spidery implement, with the curved horse-shoe clutch and the pronged lever – I could see the sharp teeth inserted quietly into the window sash, the clutch fitted to the bottom outside frame, the pressing of the lever – and my closed window was sliding quietly down, the wind and rain of Wormwood Scrubs were beating in on me again, and my paralysed eyes were looking once more down the deadly death-tube. I could see myself lying bruised and stunned in the corner, and, in imagination, could follow the murderer as he rapidly made his way back to the carriage he had issued from, and, perhaps, concealed himself under the seat, or, riding between two carriages, dropped quietly off as the train began to slow up to the station.

There were other curious contrivances, whose meaning I could not fathom, but had no doubt they all tended to the same end – the boarding of, or hanging on to, trains in motion.

I looked up at the girl.

'What do you want me to do with all these things?'

'Throw them all overboard – clothes – books – papers – everything. I have kept the only papers I need. Please get rid of them all for me.'

I did. Shannon, however, claimed the air-gun, and certainly no one who wanted it had a better right to it.

It was a wonderful weapon, the only remaining monument to the old engineer's skill. With two twists it came into three pieces, and was easily stowed in one's ordinary pockets.

The first day Shannon appeared on deck, Miss Hood being below, he tried that demon air-gun on the main-mast with a bullet of his own making. It buried itself out of sight, and a three-inch probe failed to reach it.

'No wonder it knocked the wind out of you, old man,' he said; 'if you hadn't had that breastplate on, you wouldn't be here now.'

We cleaned our memories of Old Man Hood as far as we could, as we had cleaned the ship of himself and his belongings, and Mary Hood grew brighter every day. Her burden lay behind her at the bottom of the Indian Ocean, and her sweet face was set bravely and hopefully towards the new life that awaited her in the unknown land that lay beneath the rising sun.

www.ingramcontent.com/pod-product-compliance
Lightning Source LLC
Chambersburg PA
CBHW030543180626
46810CB00005B/1984